To my granddaughter Breonna,
who inspired this story.
-LJS

For Bethany, Cassidy, and Houston
-RM

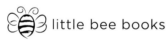 little bee books

An imprint of Bonnier Publishing USA
251 Park Avenue South, New York, NY 10010
Text copyright © 2017 by Linda Joy Singleton
Illustrations copyright © 2017 by Rob McClurkan
LITTLE BEE BOOKS is a trademark of Bonnier Publishing USA,
and associated colophon is a trademark of Bonnier Publishing USA.
Manufactured in China   HH 0917
First Edition
10 9 8 7 6 5 4 3 2 1
ISBN 978-1-4998-0396-9
Library of Congress Cataloging-in-Publication Data
Names: Singleton, Linda Joy, author. | McClurkan, Rob, illustrator. Title: Lucy loves Goosey / by Linda Joy Singleton;
illustrated by Rob McClurkan. Description: First edition. | New York, NY: Little Bee Books, [2017] Summary: When
Goosey tells Lucy they are not sisters because Lucy is a dog, Lucy tries to prove her wrong, but being herself proves
to be much more important. Identifiers: LCCN 2017003444 | Subjects: | CYAC: Geese—Fiction. | Dogs—Fiction. |
Friendship—Fiction. | Humorous stories. | BISAC: JUVENILE FICTION / Animals / Dogs. | JUVENILE FICTION /
Animals / Ducks, Geese, etc. | JUVENILE FICTION / Humorous Stories. | Classification: LCC PZ7.S6177 Luc 2017 | DDC
[E]—dc23 LC record available at https://lccn.loc.gov/2017003444

littlebeebooks.com
bonnierpublishingusa.com

LUCY LOVES GOOSEY

by Linda Joy Singleton

illustrated by Rob McClurkan

little bee books

Hey, big sister!
Watch me fly!

SPLASH!
SPLAT!
SMUSH!

Uh-oh.
Sorry, Goosey.

Go bark and dig
and chase like a dog.
I am a goose.
And you are not.

Okay,
Goosey.

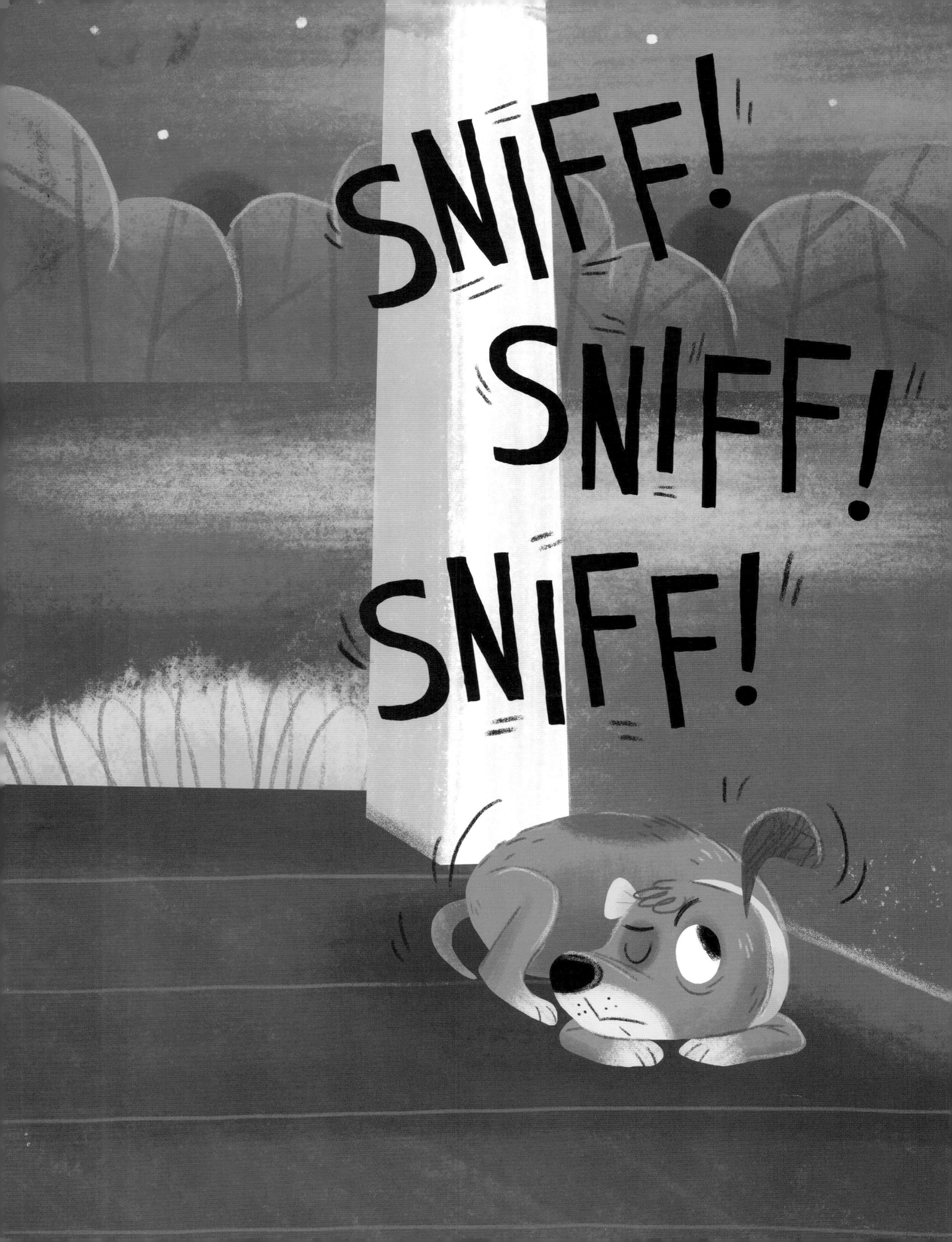
SNIFF!
SNIFF!
SNIFF!

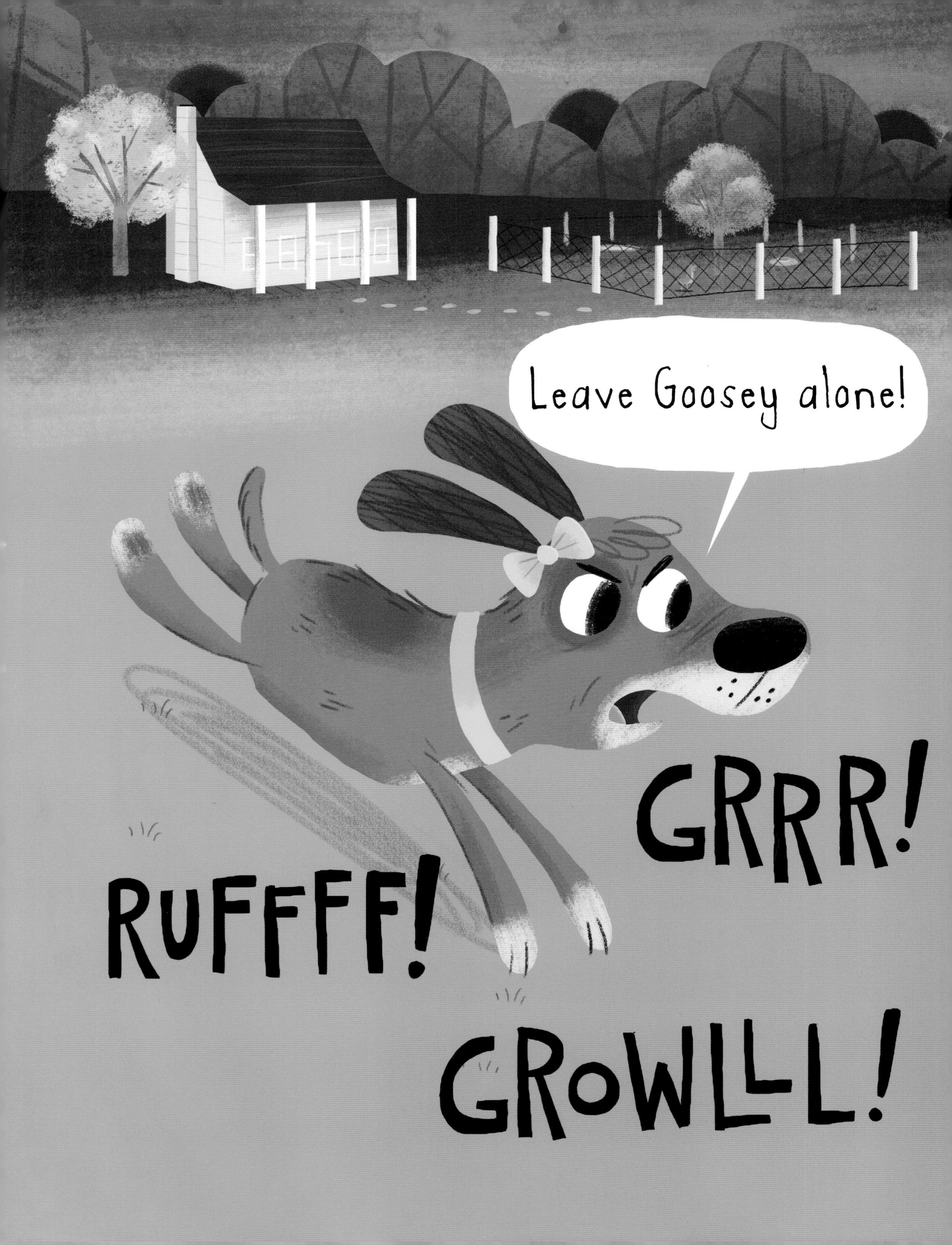
Leave Goosey alone!
GRRR!
RUFFFF!
GROWLLL!

...my friend.